Nutmeg the Guinea Pig

Ruby and Roxie the
guinea pigs — J.C.

Text copyright © 2017 by Jane Clarke and Oxford University Press
Illustrations copyright © 2017 by Oxford University Press

All rights reserved. Published by Scholastic Inc., 557 Broadway, New York,
NY 10012, *Publishers since 1920.* SCHOLASTIC and associated logos are
trademarks and/or registered trademarks of Scholastic Inc. Published
by arrangement with Oxford University Press. Series created
by Oxford University Press.

First published in the United Kingdom in 2016 by Oxford University Press,
Great Clarendon Street, Oxford, OX2 6DP.

The publisher does not have any control over and does not assume any
responsibility for author or third-party websites or their content.

No part of this publication may be reproduced, stored in a retrieval system,
or transmitted in any form or by any means, electronic, mechanical,
photocopying, recording, or otherwise, without written permission
of the publisher. For information regarding permission, write to
Oxford University Press, Rights Department, Great Clarendon Street,
Oxford, OX2 6DP, United Kingdom.

This book is a work of fiction. Names, characters, places, and incidents
are either the product of the author's imagination or are used fictitiously,
and any resemblance to actual persons, living or dead, business
establishments, events, or locales is entirely coincidental.

ISBN 978-0-545-94189-1

10 9 8 7 6 5 4 3 2 1   17 18 19 20 21

Printed in the U.S.A.   23
First printing 2017

Nutmeg the Guinea Pig

Jane Clarke

Scholastic Inc.

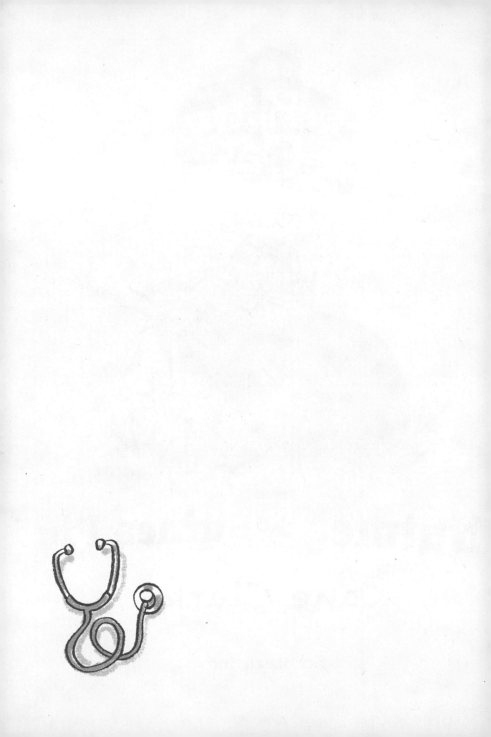

Chapter One

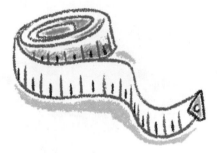

Peanut stood on his hind legs with his back against the clinic wall and stretched his whiskery nose as high as it would go.

"How big am I?" he asked as Dr. KittyCat read off the measurement on the height chart.

"Exactly three inches from nose to

toes," she told him.

"Only three?" Peanut squeaked. "Eek! I was longer than that last time I was measured. I must have shrunk!"

"Don't panic, Peanut," Dr. KittyCat meowed reassuringly. "Your tail also measures three inches. So you're six inches long in total. That's the purr-fect length for a mouse."

Peanut sighed with relief.

Dr. KittyCat smiled. "Now, are we ready for the first of our checkup days?" she asked him.

"We're ready!" Peanut scampered to the door and pulled it open. Daisy

the kitten, Basil the parakeet, Clover
the bunny, Fennel the fox cub, and
Bramble the hedgehog tumbled inside.

"Thank you for coming in today,"
Dr. KittyCat told them. "It's very

important for everyone to have regular checkups." She turned to her assistant. "Let's see all the little animals in alphabetical order, Peanut, so we don't miss anyone."

"That's a good idea." Peanut opened the *Furry First-aid Book* and took out his pencil.

"*A* . . . We don't have anyone beginning with *A*," he murmured. "*B* . . . Bramble. You must be first. Your name begins with *B* . . ." he told the little hedgehog.

"But I don't want to go first!" Bramble wailed as he rolled himself into a spiky ball.

"It won't hurt at all," Peanut reassured him. "You know how gentle Dr. KittyCat is. You're safe in her paws!"

Bramble slowly uncurled and reluctantly nodded his head.

"My name begins with a *B*, too,"
Basil piped up.

"So it does!" Peanut thought hard.
"Basil begins with a *B* followed by an A,
and Bramble begins with a *B* followed
by an *R*," he murmured. "And *A* comes
before *R*. So . . . Basil, you really should
be first!" he exclaimed. "Bramble,
Dr. KittyCat will see you second."

Bramble looked relieved as Peanut
led Basil into the examination room.

Peanut carefully wrote Basil's name
in the *Furry First-aid Book. There are so
many things to check and write down,*
he thought. *It's important I don't forget
anything.*

"First, we need to weigh you,"
he told the little parakeet.

Basil's wings flapped as he hopped
onto Dr. KittyCat's special weighing
scales. Peanut moved the weights on
the scales until they balanced.

"You weigh just over 35 grams,"

he murmured. "That's not much at all . . ." Peanut consulted the *Furry First-aid Book*. "But it's just right for a parakeet," he said, smiling.

"Now, let's measure you on the height chart."

Basil stood against the chart and stretched his beak up.

"You're bigger than me!" Peanut squeaked. He jumped on a chair so he could read off the measurement.

"Seven inches, including your tail," Peanut announced, writing it down. "That's just right for a parakeet, too."

Dr. KittyCat opened her flowery doctor's bag and took out her stethoscope.

"It's time to check your heartbeat now," she told Basil. She gently pressed her stethoscope to Basil's chest and listened carefully.

"That all sounds good," she purred. "I'll also check your breathing . . ." Dr. KittyCat listened to each side of Basil's lungs, then moved her stethoscope to his back to check again.

"Excellent," she meowed. "I can't hear any wheezes at all. Your lungs are working perfectly."

Basil proudly puffed out his fluffy chest feathers.

"The next check is a simple hearing test," Dr. KittyCat meowed. "Look this way, Basil. Peanut will help me with this test."

Peanut knew just what to do. He stood behind Basil and snapped his paws to one side of Basil's head, then the other. Basil turned his feathery head in the direction of each noise.

"Your hearing is very good," Dr. KittyCat commented.

Peanut made a quick note in the book. "The last thing is a quick eyesight check," he squeaked. He pulled out an eyesight chart and held it up. Basil quickly rattled off the names of the animals pictured on it.

"Good job, Basil," Dr. KittyCat told him. "We've finished the checkup and I'm very happy to tell you that you're very healthy. In fact, you're in excellent shape." She gave him a sticker that said: "I was a purr-fect patient for Dr. KittyCat!"

> I was a purr-fect patient for Dr. KittyCat!

"Thanks!" Basil peeped as he hopped to the door.

"I'm in excellent shape!" he proudly told the others. "There's no need to worry about the checkup: it's easy—and it doesn't take long at all!"

"That's good," yipped Fennel. "I'll be the last to go in, and I don't want to be late for Nutmeg's party. It's her birthday today, and I've been invited to her party in the park!"

"So have I," squealed Bramble and Clover together.

"And me," Daisy meowed

"Me too," peeped Basil.

Dr. KittyCat smiled. "Nutmeg is such a sweet guinea pig: She's invited everyone," she told the little animals, "and that includes me and Peanut. We're bringing the picnic!"

The little animals clapped their paws in delight.

"We'll come to the park as soon as we've finished today's checkups," Dr. KittyCat went on. "There will be plenty of time."

"I've packed the picnic basket full of yummy things," Peanut added. "It's such a beautiful summer day for a party. I can't wait, can you?!"

Chapter Two

"That's the first round of checkups completed," Peanut confirmed as he waved good-bye to Fennel and closed the clinic door. "Nutmeg, Posy, Pumpkin, Sage, and Willow will come to see us tomorrow. I've already written their names in the book in alphabetical order. And I've written down all the results of the checkups we did today."

"Good job. You're such a wonderful assistant," Dr. KittyCat purred. "I don't know what I'd do without you."

Peanut felt his ears flush with pride.

"It's wonderful to see everyone doing so well," he remarked.

"It is," Dr. KittyCat agreed. "Let's hope tomorrow's group will be just as healthy."

"We don't have to wait until tomorrow to find out," Peanut said. "Everyone will be at Nutmeg's party this afternoon."

"That reminds me," Dr. KittyCat meowed. "I should check the contents of my bag to make sure we have everything we might need in an emergency."

Peanut nodded. "Furry first-aiders have to be ready to rescue at any time!" he agreed.

Dr. KittyCat opened her flowery doctor's bag. "Scissors, syringe, medicines, ointments, instant cold packs, paw-cleaning gel, wipes," she murmured, swishing her striped tail. "Stethoscope, ophthalmoscope, thermometer, tweezers, bandages, gauze, peppermint candies, tongue depressor . . . and reward stickers. That's it!" she announced. "Everything is in here—including my knitting."

She pulled out her knitting needles and a ball of brightly colored wool. "It's such a beautiful sunny day,"

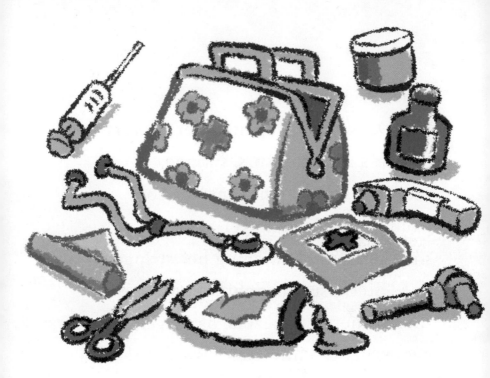

Dr. KittyCat purred contentedly. Her eyes sparkled. "I'm looking forward to relaxing in the park and making a start on a new project. This wool will make a beautiful vest."

Peanut gave a little shudder that

made his whiskers quiver. *I hope that vest isn't for me*, he thought. *I don't like that color at all!*

He glanced up at the clock.

"Eek!" he squeaked. "The party's already started. We're late!"

"Don't panic, Peanut," Dr. KittyCat meowed. "Nutmeg wants everyone to play lots of games first, then have the picnic at the end of the party. The picnic basket's already packed and in the vanbulance. We can go right now."

Dr. KittyCat's camper van, which was also an ambulance, was parked in its usual place outside the clinic. In the summer sunshine, it looked like a bright flowerbed, thanks to the flowers Peanut had painted on it.

"The vanbulance looks ready for the party!" Dr. KittyCat said, smiling. She loaded her flowery doctor's bag into the front and climbed into the driver's seat.

"I'm ready for a party, too," Peanut squeaked happily, pushing aside a bunch of birthday balloons to make room for himself on the passenger seat. "And for a picnic. I packed lots of yummy cheddar cheese. It's my favorite, and everyone else loves it, as well!"

"Yummy!" Dr. KittyCat meowed.
"Are we ready to roll?"

Peanut looked around. "Doctor's bag, *Furry First-aid Book*, picnic basket, balloons . . ." he murmured. "Oh! I forgot Nutmeg's birthday card. It's on my desk. I'll have to go back inside."

Peanut headed into the clinic.

As he opened the door, the old-fashioned telephone on his desk began to ring.

Brring! Brring!

Peanut's heart thumped as he scampered across the room and picked up the handset.

Brring!
Brring!

Who needs our help this time? he thought.

"It's Nutmeg!" panted a breathless voice on the other end of the line. "She's collapsed. Come quickly. We're at the park!"

Peanut didn't hesitate. He didn't even ask who he was talking to. "We're on our way!" he squeaked. "We'll be there in a whisker!" He slammed down the handset, grabbed Nutmeg's birthday card, and raced out to the vanbulance.

"Eek!" he squeaked as he scrambled in. "Nutmeg's collapsed! Quick! We have to get to the park!"

"What happened to her?"

Dr. KittyCat asked.

"I don't know!" Peanut gasped. He pulled in his tail and slammed the door. "I didn't wait to find out. She needs our help; it's an emergency!"

"Don't panic, Peanut," Dr. KittyCat meowed calmly. "Put on your seat belt. We're ready to roll and ready to rescue. We'll be there in a whisker!" She made sure her striped tail was out of the way, shut the door, checked the mirrors, and took her foot off the brake.

Peanut clipped in his seat belt and hit the siren button on the dashboard.

Nee-nah! Nee-nah! Nee-nah!

The vanbulance rumbled and rattled as it hurtled across Timber Bridge. The tires squealed as it rounded Duckpond

Bend. Peanut held on tight to the dashboard and tried not to squeal along, too. *Dr. KittyCat's a very safe driver,* he reminded himself. But it was no good. It scared him when she drove so fast through Thistletown. And she had to drive fast to get to Nutmeg! To keep his mind off it, he closed his eyes and tried to remember all the different kinds of cheese he had packed in the picnic basket.

Strong cheddar, mild cheddar, medium cheddar, cheddar with nuts, cheddar with onions, cheddar with cranberries, cheddar with seeds . . .

Peanut was still muttering the names of cheeses as the vanbulance screeched to a halt.

"We've arrived!" Dr. KittyCat announced as she pulled the emergency brake. Peanut opened his eyes, grabbed the *Furry First-aid Book* and Nutmeg's birthday card, and leaped out.

Posy the puppy bounded up to them. Her tail wasn't wagging like it usually did when she saw them. She looked very worried.

"Nutmeg's at the picnic spot on the other side of the playground," she yapped. "Quick, follow me!"

Chapter Three

The playground in Thistletown Park was packed with little animals having fun in the sun. Posy raced off, dodging between the slides and swings. Peanut rushed after her.

"Don't get hit by a swing!" Dr. KittyCat called. "It won't help Nutmeg if you get hurt, too!"

The words were hardly out of
Dr. KittyCat's mouth when something
thumped Peanut in the stomach so hard
that it knocked the *Furry First-aid Book*
and Nutmeg's birthday card out of his
paws and sent him flying into the air.

He landed on the hard ground with
a *whump*! Posy and Dr. KittyCat rushed
up to him.

"I-can't-breathe!" Peanut gasped.

"Crouch down with your hands
on your knees," Dr. KittyCat told him.
"That's it. You'll be fine in a minute."

Peanut bent over and caught his
breath. "What happened?" he groaned.

"You were hit by a swing and it

knocked all the breath out of you,"
Dr. KittyCat told him. "It's called being
winded! It feels very scary, but it isn't
serious. Thank goodness that swing
didn't hit you on the head! It could
have knocked you out!"

Peanut straightened up and
took a deep breath. "I can keep
going," he told Dr. KittyCat. "Nutmeg
needs us!"

"Please watch where you're going,"
Dr. KittyCat meowed as Peanut picked
up the *Furry First-aid Book* and slipped
the birthday card inside it. "Posy, slow
down a little. We don't want Peanut to
have another accident, do we?"

Posy slowed down to a trot, but
made a sudden swerve around the long
line for the ice cream truck.

"Eek!" Peanut leaped out of the
way as a squirrel on roller skates

holding an enormous ice cream whizzed toward him.

"That was close!" Dr. KittyCat murmured as Posy stopped to let them catch up with her.

"We're almost there!" Posy yapped, pointing to the edge of the baseball field. A group of little animals was gathered around a checkered picnic blanket spread out in the shade under the old oak tree.

"That's where Nutmeg collapsed. It took me a while to find a phone, but I called you as quickly as I could!" Posy said anxiously.

"You did the right thing, Posy," Dr. KittyCat told her as everyone shuffled to the side to make room for them.

The little guinea pig was lying in the middle of the picnic blanket. Her eyes were closed, and she was panting hard.

Poor Nutmeg—she looks very sick! thought Peanut, rubbing his paw across his tummy. *And I nearly had two nasty accidents that could have stopped Dr. KittyCat from treating her . . .*

It made him feel upset even thinking about it. He took Nutmeg's birthday card out of the *Furry First-aid Book* and fanned himself with it.

Dr. KittyCat knelt down beside Nutmeg. "You're safe in our paws," she reassured her. "Peanut and I will soon find out what's wrong and make you feel better. Can you tell us how you are feeling now?"

Nutmeg slowly opened her eyes and looked up.

"Ugh!" she gasped. "My lips feel all clammy. I think I'm going to be sick . . ." She closed her eyes again.

Peanut glanced toward the ice

cream truck. "Have you been eating a lot of ice cream?" he asked.

"I have!" Posy yapped. "I've had three vanilla cones already!"

"That would make me feel really sick," Peanut squeaked. "What about you, Nutmeg?"

"I—didn't—eat—any—ice—cream,"

Nutmeg panted. She sounded very out of breath.

"Has anything hit you in the stomach?" Peanut wondered.

"No!" Nutmeg puffed.

"I need to check your breathing," Dr. KittyCat told her. "Have you been stung by a wasp or anything that you might be allergic to?"

"Nooo . . ." Nutmeg gasped.

Dr. KittyCat opened her flowery doctor's bag and took out her stethoscope. She put the ends in her ears and tilted her head as she listened to Nutmeg's chest.

"I can't hear any wheezing, so

that's good. But your breathing is faster and shallower than normal. Try to breathe deeply and calmly, Nutmeg," she purred.

Peanut could see from the rise and fall of Nutmeg's chest that she was gradually slowing down each breath.

"Good job, Nutmeg," Dr. KittyCat meowed. "Your breathing is getting back to normal. That will help you feel better."

Dr. KittyCat gently took Nutmeg's paw and felt her pulse. "Your paw feels warm and your heart is beating fast," she murmured, "like you have been doing some hard exercise . . ."

Dr. KittyCat lifted her head. "Has Nutmeg been running around a lot?" she asked the little animals.

"We all have," Daisy meowed. "We've been playing baseball. It's Nutmeg's favorite game. She's very good at it. She's already scored ten runs."

Nutmeg opened her eyes again and tried to lift her head off the ground.

"Owww," she moaned. "My head aches!"

Peanut stifled an *Eek*! "She might have been hit on the head by a ball or a bat," he whispered in Dr. KittyCat's ear. "That could be really serious!"

"Take the others to one side and ask them what they saw," Dr. KittyCat told him as she carefully began to run her soft paws over Nutmeg's furry head.

Chapter Four

Peanut led the little animals out from the shade of the tree. They all squinted in the bright sunshine. Peanut shaded his eyes with his paw. "Did anyone see Nutmeg get hit on the head by a bat or a ball?" he asked them.

They all shook their heads.

"Did she bump her head on

anything? Like on the tree or the ground when she fell down?" Peanut asked.

The little animals looked at one another and shook their heads again.

"Does anyone know if she's been sick recently?" asked Peanut.

"I don't think so," said Clover, "and she seemed fine until she collapsed. It was like this . . ."

The little bunny made his legs go wobbly and he sank slowly to the ground and closed his eyes.

Peanut couldn't help smiling. "That's very well acted, and very helpful," he squeaked. "I'll tell Dr. KittyCat."

"No one saw Nutmeg get a bump on her head," Peanut reported. "And she didn't hurt her head when she collapsed. She just sort of slowly folded up and lay down."

"That's good news," Dr. KittyCat said, smiling at the little guinea pig. "I can't feel anything wrong with your head, Nutmeg. I'll check your eyes."

Peanut took the ophthalmoscope
from Dr. KittyCat's bag and handed
it to her. He watched as she carefully
examined first one eye and then the
other.

"Both pupils look normal. Your eyes look fine," she reassured Nutmeg. "You can slowly sit up now."

Peanut helped Nutmeg sit up.

"Ooh!" Nutmeg groaned. "Everything is whirling around and around."

"Lie down and rest your legs on this tree branch so they are raised higher than your head. The dizziness will soon pass," Dr. KittyCat told her.

The other little animals gathered around again, looking concerned.

"What's wrong with Nutmeg?" Bramble asked.

"We're not quite sure yet," Peanut told him.

Bramble frowned.

"There's no need to worry. We will find out what is wrong and make her better," Dr. KittyCat told everyone. "Being a first-aider is like being a detective. We examine all the clues, which we call symptoms, and find out what it is that is causing the problem. We call that the diagnosis. Sometimes, finding a diagnosis is quick and easy, but often it takes time."

"Perhaps Nutmeg's symptoms were caused by something that happened before she came to the party,"

Peanut suggested. He turned to Nutmeg.

"What were you doing this morning?" he asked her.

"I was . . . I was . . . at the clinic," Nutmeg replied. She sounded very woozy.

"But it wasn't your turn at the clinic," Peanut squeaked. "Your name begins with an N so you're in the second group. You're coming for your checkup tomorrow."

"Am I?" Nutmeg sounded puzzled. "Oh yes, that's right. Today's my birthday, isn't it?"

"It is! You have lots of birthday

cards to open," said Peanut. He added their card to the pile on the picnic blanket.

"Nutmeg is a bit muddled," Dr. KittyCat murmured. "Confusion is another symptom that will help us with our diagnosis."

Peanut made a quick note in the record book. *I always feel dizzy and woozy when I go on a swing and put my head back,* he thought. *If Nutmeg spent a lot of time playing on the swings, that might account for it.*

"Do you remember Nutmeg going on the swings?" Peanut asked her friends. "Or on anything else that might make her dizzy, like the merry-go-round?"

The little animals shook their heads again.

"Nutmeg just wanted us to play baseball," Willow the duckling quacked. "It's her birthday so we all agreed to play whatever game she chose."

"We've been playing for a long time," Clover said, taking off his sun hat and fanning himself with it. "It's such a hot sunny day, too, it's hard to be furry and play in this heat. I thought my ears would boil . . ."

"It's hard to run around in the sun even if you don't have fur," Willow quacked. "My feet felt as if they were on fire!"

"The heat made my tongue hang out," Posy added. "I couldn't stop panting for ages—and I only ran the bases three times. Nutmeg ran them more than that!"

Dr. KittyCat looked at Peanut. "Pass me the thermometer, please," she told him. "I'm going to take your temperature, Nutmeg."

Peanut delved into Dr. KittyCat's flowery doctor's bag. He fitted a fresh hygiene cover onto the thermometer and handed it to Dr. KittyCat, who gently inserted it into Nutmeg's ear. They waited for the *beep, beep, beep*.

"Just as I thought," Dr. KittyCat murmured. "Nutmeg's temperature is slightly raised, but I think I know why that is the case."

"She isn't coming down with an infectious disease, is she?" Peanut asked nervously.

"I don't think so," meowed Dr. KittyCat. "All the symptoms point to a different diagnosis."

"Don't worry, Nutmeg," she told the little guinea pig. "We'll soon have you feeling well again. I've figured out what is wrong with you!"

Chapter Five

Everyone looked at Dr. KittyCat.

"I just need to check one more thing," Dr. KittyCat meowed. "Nutmeg usually wears her hat. Does anyone know where it is?"

Peanut was puzzled. *Nutmeg's hat?* he thought. *What has that got to do with her feeling sick?*

"It's over there!" Daisy pointed across the baseball field to what looked like a little heap of material.

"What's it doing over there?" Peanut asked.

"At the start of the game, Nutmeg took off her hat and used it to mark first base," Daisy explained. "I'll get it."

She scampered off and returned with Nutmeg's hat dangling from one of her claws. She handed it to Peanut.

"Owww!" he squeaked. It was so hot from lying in the sun that he almost dropped it!

It was as if a lightbulb had gone off inside his head. Peanut suddenly knew what was wrong with Nutmeg, too!

"Nutmeg took off her sun hat," he squeaked excitedly. "She's not used to being in the sun without it, and she ran around a lot. She's had too much sun. She has a mild case of heat exhaustion!"

"Good job, Peanut," Dr. KittyCat meowed. "Mild heat exhaustion is my diagnosis, as well.

"Poor Nutmeg; no wonder you feel so sick." Dr. KittyCat gently placed the guinea pig's sun hat back on her furry head. "But now that we have the right diagnosis, we know exactly how to treat you," she went on. "It's a simple treatment. We just need to cool you down, give you something to drink, and give you some peace and quiet."

"The vanbulance is the best place for that: We can put the fans on full blast," Peanut squeaked.

"But I don't want to leave my party!" Nutmeg cried. A tear trickled down her furry cheek.

"Cheer up, Nutmeg," murmured Sage the owlet. "The vanbulance is very special. Going in it is a great birthday treat!"

"I'm sure Nutmeg will soon feel well enough to come back to her party," Dr. KittyCat told the little animals. "But we don't want anyone else becoming sick from too much sun. You should all have a drink of water and a little rest in the shade while we are gone."

The little animals nodded their agreement.

Dr. KittyCat and Peanut helped Nutmeg to the vanbulance. Once inside, Peanut turned on the fan and closed the polka-dotted curtains. Soon it felt nice and cool.

"It's like being in a beautiful shady garden," Nutmeg sighed as she settled down on the bench seat beside the table.

Peanut filled a bowl with cold water from the tap over the little sink.

"Ooh, that feels good!" Nutmeg gave a little squeal as Peanut gently sponged her fur with cold water.

Dr. KittyCat filled three glasses of water. "One for each of us," she murmured. "It's important for everyone to remember to have plenty to drink on such a hot sunny day."

She added a sprinkle of salt to Nutmeg's glass and handed it to the damp little guinea pig. "Too much sun makes you very dry inside and out," she explained. "And as you dry out you lose salts from your body. The medical term for that is dehydration. You need to sip this slowly to replace the water and salt you have lost."

"It doesn't taste very nice." Nutmeg wrinkled her nose.

"I know," Dr. KittyCat meowed. "But it will make you feel a lot better."

"I feel much better already." Nutmeg smiled.

"You'll feel like a new guinea pig after a drink and a short rest," Dr. KittyCat promised.

"You can lie down in my room, if you like," Peanut told her, pointing to a little cabin just under the roof. "I'll pull down the rope ladder for you."

Nutmeg finished her drink and climbed up to Peanut's room. "This is great!" she exclaimed as she pulled the cabin curtains closed.

Peanut glugged down his water and opened the *Furry First-aid Book*. The breeze from the fan wafted through Peanut's whiskers as he began to write up his notes on Nutmeg's case. It felt very refreshing.

It wasn't long before Nutmeg opened the curtains and poked her whiskery nose out of Peanut's cabin.

"I've been thinking," she told them. "I'll only need a very quick checkup when I come to the clinic tomorrow— I've had such a thorough birthday checkup today!"

"You have!" laughed Peanut and Dr. KittyCat as Nutmeg climbed down.

"Thank you for letting me use your room," she told Peanut. "It's fun being in the vanbulance. Sage was right. It *is* a birthday treat!"

"And here's another one," Dr. KittyCat meowed, handing her a sticker that said: "I was a purr-fect patient for Dr. KittyCat!"

Nutmeg gave a big smile as she

stuck the sticker on her hat. "I don't
feel sick or dizzy anymore, and my
headache's gone!" she announced. "I'm
ready to go back to my party! It will be
picnic time soon!"

I was a
purr-fect
patient for
Dr. KittyCat!

Chapter Six

Peanut and Dr. KittyCat heaved
the heavy picnic basket out of the
vanbulance. Peanut balanced
Dr. KittyCat's bag and the *Furry
First-aid Book* on top of it.

"Nutmeg, can you help by carrying
the bunch of balloons?" he asked. "There
are enough for everyone to take one

home with them, and there will still be
some left over to play with."

Nutmeg gave a little skip. "I'd love
to!" she squealed.

She led the way, holding so many
balloons that, for a moment, Peanut
thought she might take off into the sky.

"Watch where you're going, Peanut!" Dr. KittyCat reminded him.

Peanut kept a careful lookout for swings and slides and squirrels on roller skates as they crossed the playground. He breathed a sigh of relief as he helped Dr. KittyCat set the basket down on the picnic blanket. Everyone was safe—and everyone was very pleased to see them.

"Nutmeg! I'm so glad you're back! You look so much better!" Posy yapped, wagging her tail so hard that her whole body wiggled.

"I'm feeling better, too!" Nutmeg smiled as her friends helped her tie the balloons to the tree so they wouldn't blow away.

"Would you like to play another game of baseball before we have the picnic?" Daisy asked her.

"Ooh, yes!" Nutmeg squealed.

"Take it easy, Nutmeg," Dr. KittyCat warned. "If you run around in this heat you might feel sick again." She settled down in the shade and took her knitting out of her flowery doctor's bag.

Nutmeg sat down. "Dr. KittyCat's right," she told her friends. "I've done enough running around in

the sun today. I'm happy to sit here next to Dr. KittyCat and watch her knit. I'd like to learn how to do that one day. Maybe Peanut would like to take my place on the team?"

"I would!" Peanut squeaked excitedly. "I haven't played a game of baseball since I was in school. I used to be good at it, too!"

"Then you can go first," Daisy meowed. She handed him the bat.

Peanut scampered across the baseball field and took up his position. It was quite a big bat for a little mouse. He gave it an experimental swish.

"I'm ready," he squeaked.

Posy was pitching. She took a long run-up and threw the ball as hard as she could.

"Eek!" Peanut squeaked as the ball whizzed toward him. He took an enormous swing and—*whack!*—the bat hit the ball. *Wheee!* The ball rocketed toward the old oak tree.

"Watch out!" Peanut called to Dr. KittyCat, but it was too late.

The ball hit the tree trunk, popped a balloon, and landed with a plop in Dr. KittyCat's lap. It rolled onto the ground.

She leaped to her feet, dropping her knitting. Peanut's mouth fell open.

"Don't just stand there," Basil peeped. "Drop the bat and run!"

Peanut scampered around the bases. Everyone jumped up and down and clapped their paws and wings.

"Did you see that?" Peanut rushed over to Dr. KittyCat and Nutmeg. "I scored a home run!" he squeaked, waving his arms around and jumping up and down with excitement.

"Peanut, your back paw is caught in Dr. KittyCat's knitting," Nutmeg warned him.

"Is it?" Peanut whirled around, taking the wool with him. Dr. KittyCat's knitting fell off her knitting needles. "Eek! It's unraveling!" Peanut squeaked.

"Oh dear," Dr. KittyCat meowed. "I was knitting that for you . . . Never mind, I hadn't gotten very far. Nutmeg, would you like these knitting needles and this wool as a birthday present? I'll teach you how to knit."

"Yes, please!" Nutmeg squealed.

"Maybe we should have the picnic first?" Peanut suggested as Dr. KittyCat wound her wool back into a ball.

The little animals looked on excitedly as Peanut helped Dr. KittyCat unpack the picnic.

"Cucumber sandwiches, corn on the cob, and cheese, cheese, cheese, cheese, cheese . . ." Peanut announced proudly, ". . . and a big seedy cake with candles, of course! Happy birthday, Nutmeg!"

Nutmeg squealed with delight.

"Thanks, Peanut. You and Dr. KittyCat
have helped to make it such a special
day!"

Peanut smiled from ear to ear as

he helped Nutmeg open her cards and cut the cake. What an exciting day it had been. He'd scored a home run, too! *Every day is special when you're a furry first-aider,* he thought.

The end

Dr. KittyCat's guide to

Here is some advice from Dr. KittyCat on how to stay safe while out in the sun.

Wear a sun hat

Wearing a sun hat is a great way of protecting your head, face, and neck from the sun's rays, keeping you cool and helping to stop you from getting burned. The brim will also shade your eyes from the bright glare of the sun. Just ask Nutmeg!

staying safe in the sun!

Apply sunscreen

Just because you're wearing a hat doesn't mean you don't need to put on lots of sunscreen, too! Make sure you put it on before you go outside, so that it can start to protect your skin properly as soon as you're in the sun. Reapply it often, and ALWAYS right away after you've been swimming.

Drink plenty of water

When it's hot Dr. KittyCat always drinks lots of water, even if she doesn't feel thirsty, so that she stays hydrated. She also stays in the shade as much as possible, which is the best way to stay cool!

Dr. KittyCat is ready to rescue:
Willow the Duckling

"My heart was thumping so hard I couldn't breathe and my knees knocked together and my feathers shook all over. Then the room started spinning. I thought I was going to choke!"

"Poor Willow, you definitely had a panic attack," Dr. KittyCat murmured sympathetically. "A panic attack feels very, very scary, but it's all over now."

"It was horrible!" Willow quacked.
"I don't think I'll ever dare to get
onstage again." Her feathers drooped.
"I'll miss the talent show, and
I practiced so hard for it. It took me
forever to learn my dance."

Don't
panic,
Peanut!

A note from the author:
Jane says . . .

"Roxie and Ruby the rescue
guinea pigs didn't like having
a bath and their
toenails clipped,
but they loved being
wrapped in a towel
and fed dandelion
leaves afterward."

See you next time!